Surviving Our Extinction: The Chronicles of Esther

By Jeff S. Long

Published by Madrigal Books

October 2015

Rev. 12

Thanks to everyone for the support on this project.

I'd like to thank Bryan Kneiding for coming up with the name of Esther and some other story elements.

I'd also like to thank Alyssa White for working with me on the cover design and my wife Lily for posing for it.

Lastly, I'd like to thank my daughter Brittany for militantly proof-reading this manuscript and unabashedly pointing out hundreds of punctuation, grammar, and continuity errors. I am humbled. Some verbiage I wrote stylistically, knowing it didn't follow proper grammar rules.

Dedicated to my wife Lily, and our children Brittany, Brenna, Andrea, and Ryan. I love you so much.

Table of Contents

DAY 1 5

DAY 2 7

DAY 3 11

DAY 4 17

DAY 5 24

DAY 6 32

DAY 7 40

DAY 8 49

DAY 9 60

DAY 10 67

DAY 11 76

DAY 12 83

DAY 13 94

DAY 14 105

DAY 15 111

DAY 19 114

Epilogue 116

DAY 1

I am writing in my diary for the first time since I got it for Christmas four years ago. I think I need to, because something really strange is going on and I'm stuck here in my room anyways.

I'll explain, but first the basics.

My name is Esther. I'm 16 years old. I live in the small mountain community of Pine Ridge. My dad is the pastor of our local church, and my mom works in administration for the town. My brother's name is Tommy. He's 5.

For I guess two weeks now, my parents have been turning the channel to watch stuff on the news. I hate when I miss my shows for the stupid news! I haven't really paid attention, but I know it's something my parents are really concerned about. This week they took us out of school and told me to stay in my room. Tommy is staying in his.

Now the power is out, and the phone is dead too so I can't even get a hold of my friends to see what they know. I'm really scared. Dad is doing some sort of remodeling. I can hear him downstairs hammering at all hours. Is this really the time? Maybe there's some sort of big storm approaching.

I can see people out my window hanging around outside and even in our backyard, as if there's some sort of party, which makes no sense if there is some crisis. I'm not allowed out of my room except to use the restroom. They are bringing us meals. I keep asking Mom to tell me what's going on, but she won't.

She just tells me to pray.

Esther

DAY 2

I am having trouble writing. I am having trouble doing *everything*: my hands are so cut up. I think there's still glass in my right hand. It's been a terrible day, the worst in my life.

This morning there was suddenly a lot of banging and yelling going on downstairs. I was just lying in my room reading a book. Then I heard my mother scream. I sat up in my bed, and right then Tommy burst into my room, flinging the door aside. Dad was right behind him. But something was wrong with Dad. He was, I don't know, like he was out of his mind. He grabbed Tommy and bit him on the shoulder, really hard. At first I thought he was trying to hug him. I was so shocked I didn't know what to do, and I fell backwards off my bed.

When Dad looked up, he had this blank, hateful stare. He looked right at me but it was like he was somebody else. He still had some of Tommy's blood in his mouth. My God!

Right then, behind him, Mom, running into the room yelled, "Get out now!"

Tommy was writhing in pain, and slowly backed into me. His little hand grabbed my shirt and he held on tight. Dad paused for a moment, and then lunged at me.

I yelled "Daddy, please!" but he didn't say anything.

I staggered backward and then out of nowhere Mom hit him on the head with something, maybe a frying pan or something like that. I didn't understand what was going on, but this really freaked me out. Dad fell towards me and I shrieked. He landed right on top of Tommy. God, I was still in shock, I don't know what made me act. I pulled Tommy out from under him and to his feet. But the next thing I know, Dad is moving again, and trying to bite Tommy's leg. We had to get away right *now*. It was like he was trying to kill us! I smashed the window with my elbow. Parts of it didn't fall out but when Dad got up he was blocking our way out, and I knew we had one last chance, so I held onto Tommy tight and threw us both through the window. The last thing I saw was Mom's face. She was raising the frying pan in the air again.

We rolled down the roof, fell off the end and hit the ground hard. I landed on Tommy, poor thing. I got up and grabbed him and we ran into the wash behind our house as fast as we could and didn't look back.

My hands were bleeding so badly from them going through the window that I had to take off my shirt and wrap my hands. Tommy helped me. I was cold in just my bra and sweatpants but I knew I had to stop the bleeding. Tommy is worse than I am. His shoulder hurts and he's very weak. The fall and me landing on him must have hurt him more than I thought. I think we should stay here in the woods until morning and see what happens. I haven't heard sirens or commotion or anything to believe someone is coming to our rescue.

Tommy and I curled up together under a tree. We were both so cold and hungry and tired. I finally have time to think and write this. It's a good thing I had my little diary in

my pocket. But what I wouldn't do to trade
it for a blanket or a candy bar!

Daddy! My Daddy! What happened to you?
Daddy I love you.

Oh Mommy! Are you OK? I feel terrible for
leaving her there. I need to get the police!
But I am so exhausted I need to sleep first.

What is happening to us? I don't
understand. Maybe Dad has rabies or
something? I heard this causes you to go
crazy. Maybe it's all over town and that's
why they had us stay in our rooms. We
should be careful if we meet other people.

This is just a horrible, horrible nightmare.
God help us.

Esther

DAY 3

I didn't sleep at all last night. I mostly just cried. Tommy's still sleeping. He hasn't moved in hours. Good, he needs it. I think we should go back home and see what's going on. Maybe there will be paramedics there. Maybe Dad got some help. Whatever this thing is, it's bad, I know that, and I know we didn't do anything to deserve what happened too. I'll write more later. Before I get Tommy up, I want to look around and see if anybody's around…

HELP ME!

HELP ME! Make this end. I'M A YOUNG GIRL. I'm supposed to be dealing with hair and makeup and school and boys and NOT THIS.

Oh my God, there's no way. There's no way this is happening. God help me please I can't do this, I just can't do this. Somebody, anybody, please help me.

I will try to regain my composure. I don't know if I can, this is too much. I think I've cried all a person can cry. I will try to write what happened.

I looked around the area we slept and didn't see anyone. When I came back Tommy was gone.

No! I can't. I can't write this. It's too horrible!

After calming down, I think I can write this. I need to, for my own sanity, I think.

Tommy was gone. I started looking for him and then I saw him standing out in the clearing sort of staring into space facing away from me. I walked over and called his name and he turned and looked at me and God help me he had the same hateful blank stare Dad did…. and then he came at me! He was…snarling. I've never heard anything like that in my life. He jumped on me, knocked me over. I pushed him off of me but he turned and grabbed my leg and tried to bite me. I pulled my leg away and he turned and looked at me and puked blood on the ground, or at least that's what it looked like. At this point I knew whatever Dad had Tommy had. I tried to get up and run but he grabbed my leg again and pulled me down. Then I did the unthinkable. God forgive me I did the hardest thing I've ever had to do in my entire life.

I reached for a nearby rock and smashed him on the head. He stopped for a moment, but then let out a loud snarl and tried to bite me again. I hit him again as hard as I could and blood splattered all over my legs. I got up and backed up and turned and ran.

I just ran. I just ran and ran until my lungs were on fire and then I ran some more. I ran until I was out of the wash and back on Main Street. There was no-one around, no cars, no nothing, and I just collapsed at the side of the road. At that moment I half wished the Earth would just swallow me up.

Eventually I got up and decided to walk into town. At this point I couldn't care less who sees me in just my bra. I'm half covered in blood anyway. There was no-one there. Nobody, nothing. Some of the shops were boarded up. Some cars were crashed or parked funny. Tom's Bakery had been broken into. Who breaks into a donut shop? Maybe people are hungry like I am. I went in and grabbed some donuts and stuffed my pocket with bread too. I've never stolen a thing in my life, but when you haven't eaten in a day you start to think differently. God the sugar was a rush. I went over to the rec center and there was no-one there either. Well, there was…a body.. in the hallway. Didn't recognize the person, he …or she…was half missing and covered in blood- almost black at this point. Sick. Just sickening. It looks like the person had been in a car wreck…or something, gross. I wonder if that's what happens to someone who doesn't get away from someone who has this sickness, whatever it is.

I found a rack of golf shirts at the Pro Shop and put two of them on. If we had to, we could stay here instead of the wash, it would be much warmer.

…We….

That's right, Tommy is … I shudder to think…and…I'm all alone now. I really am alone.   There's no-one here.

I decided to go back to the wash and see if I could see Tommy from a distance and talk to him somehow. So I went back down into the wash via the trail we always use but he wasn't there. I continued on the trail over to a nearby cul-de-sac and several houses were empty. I picked one. Nobody was there either. I found a crowbar under the deck and pried the front door open, which was tough as there's a tree in front of it. The power was out there too and luckily the alarm was off. Not that it would have stopped me. I stole some more food: Some beer, some ginger snaps. I also found a portable radio and turned it on.

That's where I learned about what is going on. Brad King was on the air on KPRR in some sort of loop explaining about the virus and the epidemic. I know what they're called now. Zombies. What a terrible name, but it makes sense, like in the Voodoo religion. Now I know the world, or at least Pine Ridge, is rampant with this virus, and the people are clearly losing. The broadcast speaks of some sort of compound where people are going for safety. I have to find this place. I have to see if there's a cure for Tommy and Dad, and probably Mom too at this point. I have to find it or I'm going to die. I'm going to die of starvation or by the hand one of those things who were once people I knew. Either that or I'm going to die of insanity, or possibly, loneliness.

In the middle ages the black plague killed one-third to one-half of the population. They went to church to pray and hold hands and contaminated each other in the process, dooming their families back home. We know about germs now. I learned about germs in science class. Tommy got the virus because he got bit. Dad got it somehow, probably the same way. I can go to this compound and be with other people who aren't infected, and we can ride this out. I want to live. I WANT TO LIVE!

I sat and had my first beer ever. It was an IPA whatever that is. Gross. But I really needed to calm down. Then I woke up. I guess I was exhausted, and had fallen asleep. It's almost dark. I think I'll stay here tonight. Can tomorrow be worse than today? I don't see how. But at least I know what's going on now and I have a plan.

Esther

DAY 4

I slept a little, at least until I heard gunshots in the middle of the night. That scared me a lot, but I bet it's someone defending themselves. I had crawled, believe it or not, underneath the kitchen sink into the cabinet and slept there. I was afraid I was too exposed to sleep anywhere else. If they can get into my boarded up house, they can get in here, and I didn't want to be found. Damn that kitchen was small. I lay there for a moment and just thought. Am I all alone in this? Where is everyone? Why is no-one coming to the rescue? Maybe they can't for some reason. Maybe everyone is fighting to stay alive themselves? Maybe they're all dead or worse, one of those…zombies. But what about things like the military? Where are they?

I took a sponge bath in the kitchen. I didn't want to take a real bath or make any noise in case it attracted zombies but I wanted to get all that blood off me because I think it might have infected me if I got it in a cut or something. Poor Tommy, it was so hard to wash off my little brother's blood. I still can't believe I'm the one that did that to him, although according to Brad King's radio broadcast you can't kill a zombie unless you destroy the brain. How bizarre. So maybe Tommy's still out there and maybe I can find a cure.

I wanted to find warmer clothes but I just found a pair of pants with huge holes in the knees. They were too big anyway. I found a backpack and put in as much food as I could. The refrigerator food had gone bad. Of the non-perishable food I could find there was more dog food than human food, but I was grateful for what was there. I went over to the front door to peer out and see who or what might be around, but nobody was there. I bent down and picked up the crowbar I had left there when breaking in. I held it in my hands and swung it around a little. I realized something right then. I can't be Esther anymore, not on the outside. I have to be someone else now. I have to be Lara Croft. Actually, I have to be Sarah Connor. Until things get better I am no longer a princess. I no longer care about when my hair was washed last or what some guy said to his friend about me in class. I no longer care about food expiration dates or eating something off the ground. I'm in survival mode now. I have to do what it takes to stay alive. I swung the crowbar around a bit more, and I picked up a big screwdriver I found in a toolbox. I know how to swing a crowbar if I have to. It's heavy, but I can do it. I can stab with this screwdriver. I don't know how far away this compound is, but it may be days and I want to be prepared. I can't believe I have to be this person. I don't like what I see in the mirror. I want to live though, of that I am sure.

I set off into the woods east of the house I stayed at, and followed the creek south. I was proud of myself for knowing I should stay by water. As I hiked up the creek carefully, I saw a blond-haired man in his mid-forties standing in his back yard. He didn't see me. I crouched quietly. I think he's one of them, he's just wandering. I looked carefully through the bushes. Then I saw for sure he was a zombie. He was definitely wandering and moaning quite a bit too. I need to learn the behavior of these things if I'm going to stay alive.

Eventually he wandered east and so I quietly went west towards the street and there I saw in front of me a house that seemed fenced in, boarded-up, and fortified. I don't know if this is the compound I heard about or not, but it's very close to where I started out, and it's better than being in a regular house or in the woods! Can I get this lucky?

I didn't see any more zombies so I crept up to the driveway of the house. There was a pile of bodies that had apparently been burned recently; it was still smoldering. I waited to make sure nothing moved. I figured it must be zombies who were brain-killed by uninfected people. God the smell! I was about to call out towards the house to see if anyone would answer when I noticed that at the top of the pile of bodies was the body of a little boy.

I stopped, stared, and shrieked as I fell to my knees. NO!

Immediately I heard very loud growls or snarls or whatever all around me and bushes were rustling and I didn't have time to do anything, but get up and run. I ran up to the gate and pounded on it.

"For God's sake, let me in. LET ME IN!
Now! Come on, COME ON, they're after
me."

Then after what seemed like forever, I heard
a recorded female voice with a heavy
Russian accent. "Stow your weapon, and
keep hands in air, or you will be shot."

The growling was getting closer. I could
hear them running at me at full gait. I dared
not look back.

"LET ME IN DAMMIT. Let me in
RIGHT NOW DO YOU HEAR ME?! I'm
not a zombie and they're after me! LET ME
IN LET ME IN."

I banged on the gate but nothing happened.
I turned to see a man zombie sprinting
towards me, his face bloody. Then I heard a
buzzing sound and the gate moved open in
front of me and I fell inward. I tried to
stand up and shut the gate but the zombie
was too fast and slammed the gate into me.
He growled at me so loud it was deafening.
I shoved back on the gate and grabbed my
screwdriver. I took a deep breath and swung
hard towards its head. The zombie groaned

and his head dropped downward. I scrambled up and shoved hard on the gate, pushing the zombie, my screwdriver still in his head, outward. He fell backward and I shut the gate. I just stood there and stared at it through the fence, panting.

I just stared.

It didn't get up, but others were coming, and coming quickly. Even though I was behind the fenced-in gate, I had to get inside.

Without thinking I opened the gate, reached forward, pulled my screwdriver out of his head, slammed the gate shut, turned, and ran up the causeway. There was a sign that said I had to put my hands in the air, so I did that on the way to the front door. The door was locked.

I knocked but nobody answered.

I knocked again and yelled "I can kill a zombie! LET ME IN!"

Through the front door, I heard a person, the same female Russian voice I heard from the loudspeaker.

"So you can kill zombie. So what? I am think you will do that tomorrow and day after and every day now on. We should not let you in, unless you help enough to support yourself and even more, every day."

"I will, I will," I yelled.

I didn't know if I really could, but I was going to try. What choice did I have?

The door unlatched and opened slowly, and I walked in.

Esther

DAY 5

I slept fairly well, FINALLY. I still awoke to the sounds of gunfire several times during the night. The first time I sat up and looked around to see people working and running around the place with guns. I felt fairly safe and went back to sleep each time. I have hope again. It's an amazing thing to have hope. It's one thing to want to live; it's another to want to live with the idea that there is a tomorrow that I can look forward to.

I definitely found the compound. The girl who let me in introduced herself as Oksana. She was indeed the recorded voice I heard on the way in. She introduced me to her fiancé Jack, his daughter from a previous marriage Bridgett, and a host of other people including Brad King, the radio personality of KPRR from the FM broadcast I heard earlier, and his girlfriend Jenny. Many people have made it here. It's no panacea though. Supplies are low and everyone here has lost family members. Jack owns the house, so he is calling the shots by default, but I hear that he hasn't really taken leadership yet officially.

This place is amazing. When did they do all this? It's no longer a house, it's like a Girl Scout camp.

Oksana has turned me over to John for training, but she has taken me under her wing at night, and I have also made friends with Bridgett. I got to meet her briefly before going to see John. She says she has a younger sister named Brenda who was around somewhere. I hope I get to meet her soon.

John was really nice too. He introduced himself by giving me a flower. "A beautiful flower for a beautiful girl," he said.

He's training me to use a shotgun. "Aim for their heads. Get a good line, close your eyes and squeeze the trigger."

I am told my assigned duties will be to do what they call "reconnaissance", which sounds fancy, but really I'm just going back into town and getting… stealing… supplies. It's actually a more dangerous job than Patrol. Those people assigned to the job of patrol go around and around the outside of the compound on shifts. I wonder if they're the ones that collect and burn the bodies? At night I am going to cook and clean. How can I work all day and all night too? That's crazy. I don't start that stuff until tomorrow though. They gave me a temporary job today.

After an exhausting day of reloading shotgun shells, I collapsed on a bunk bed they assigned me on the back deck. It's outside, but it's covered by the balcony above. The back deck has many bunk beds, benches, tables, and big metal drums with fires in them. There's a rack of metal shelves on one side full of water bottle pallets. The whole back deck is surrounded with 10 feet high boards with barbed wire and alarm lights on top of that. I feel pretty safe. I am so tired.

 Oksana came over and sat down with me.

"How are you this day?"

I told her I was fine, but really I wasn't. Every time I have down time I think of my family. I think of Tommy.

"What did you used to do…before…this?"
I asked her.

"I used to be nurse in hospital. I help
children mostly. Now there are no more
children live, and no more for future."

If she was trying to cheer me up, it wasn't
working. This probably wasn't the time, but
I still was unsure what to make of my life
now. Is this it?

"What do you have to look forward to?" I
asked her.

Oksana was very cheerful at hearing this.
"Jack and I decide to marry, in a few days
from now, in case we have no more chance.
It is big thing for me. How about you?"

"I don't have anything to look forward to
but living I guess," I said. "I wanted to help
my brother Tommy, but… now I can look
forward to your wedding. Who is marrying
you, and where?"

"We're getting marry here of course"
Oksana sounded even more upbeat. "I

understand your father was priest. Pravda? Can you marry us like him?"

"He was a pastor, and I can't officially marry anybody," I told her.

"Will you do anyway?" she asked.

"Sure!" I half-smiled, and she smiled back.

"Mena raduyet! It is set then".

Oksana then got serious. "Tomorrow, you on my team with John. We do recon mission."

I asked her if I would be holding my own if I did these jobs like she said I had to.

She said, "Getting supplies is important job. We need food, water, medicine, ammunition, and small creature comfort to help people be happy. If we fail at this, it hurt everybody here."

I guess that answered my question.

"What you doing?" she asked.

"I'm just going to take a nap."

"Nyet. No you're not," she said, "Not yet. You need two weapon lesson a day, one in morning, one at night. This lesson is real deal. Grab your shotgun and meet John on west balcony."

I didn't mind. I really did want to fit in.

John greeted me with a smile. "Hi there sweetie," he said

He sure is nice. John used to work at a gun store, so he knows his guns, even though he's only 22, I think he said.

"Ok so you're on for just an hour this time." John was all business now. "Use your binoculars and watch for signals from the guys watching the security cameras. There seem to be more and more zombies each day."

I looked through the scope and searched. "Do I shoot ones just walking around or only ones trying to get in?" I asked.

John continued his instruction, "We need to conserve ammo sweetheart, so shoot the ones trying to get in, but if you take another one out, nobody's going to mind."

I sat there and John shot zombies. I finally decided to shoot at one, an older man. I figured he didn't have much family. At least that's what I convinced myself of. I pulled the trigger and his brains went all over the tree behind him. Then he dropped. I stared at his not-moving body for a long time, contemplating the meaning of what I was doing, for me, for him. I finally went back to searching when several zombies started to bang on the south wall all at once. They were definitely trying to get in. I looked through my scope and could see seven zombies, including two women. John was taking them out as I watched. I didn't want him to think I wasn't contributing so I picked out a woman to shoot and ....wait. She looked familiar. I looked through the binoculars instead of the scope and ...it was my mom. I looked over at John and he was lining them up.

"Don't shoot the blond woman," I pleaded, "She's my mom."

John stopped his zeroing-in and looked over at me. "Esther, it has to be done."

I didn't say anything but my eyes were pleading with him still. He didn't say anything and I finally said "PLEASE?" He just looked at me. I closed my eyes and covered my ears.

Then I heard the shot.

Esther

DAY 6

Oksana came by again last night when I was getting some sleep, or what they call "rack time" around here. She brought Jack with her this time. It was my first time really talking to him.

He shook my hand and said, "It's good to have you Esther, and I'm thrilled you will marry us, you're the closest thing we have to someone from the clergy."

I'm not sure I have the same faith I once had considering the hellish, horrific circumstances we are now dealing with, but I'm not going to rain on their parade.

Oksana then got down to business. "This is first recon mission for you, Esther, are you ready for it? Are your hands heal OK?"

I nodded. I was nervous. Going outside again with those things is not something I was looking forward to. "Honestly I'm not sure I'm the best person for this job."

"Not true!" Oksana retorted. "You'll do just fine. I seen you shoot and I seen how you handle yourself at gate before."

I resigned myself to dealing with it.

"Then bring your shotgun, no need for a scope, we'll see you at sun-up." Jack said. He kissed Oksana, smiled, and walked away.

I can tell how much they love each other. Sometimes you can see it in people's eyes and in their smiles.

I asked Oksana, "Should I bring my screwdriver, crowbar, or knife?"

"Bring anything you want that you can stash in clothes and not carry with hands."

That meant I could take my screwdriver. I drifted off to sleep, not sure what the day would bring.

Just before daybreak I heard screaming out front. I'm used to the constant moaning, although it's getting worse, but screaming is not something I hear all the time. People were running around. I sat up in my bunk and decided to get up early to see what was going on. By the time I got to the front door it was open and an exhausted man and a woman were escorted in by Patrol. They collapsed on the floor.

"Get them some water and make sure they have no open wounds," Brad yelled.

There were so many people I stayed back. Apparently they are married and their names are Michael and Rose.

"Who was screaming?" I asked Brad when things settled. He just looked at me and said, "Later."

I ate some oatmeal and a small can of peas, put on some new clothes, and grabbed my gear. I met John and Oksana at the front door. Patrol cleared us and we sneaked down to the gate and out. I was so scared I can't even tell you.

John hot-wired one of the abandoned cars nearby and we drove down into town. I could not believe the mess on the roads everywhere we went. We got into town and I was amazed to see the rec center had burned to the ground. Wow. No fire response, nobody there to do anything, just a burned smoldering building sitting there. We passed several zombies on the way in the woods, and ran over one too.

John laughed and said, "Saves us a bullet!"

I didn't think it was so funny but I kept my mouth shut. He's nice, but his lack of empathy sometimes scares me. However, I care a lot less about his lack of empathy when my life is in immediate danger.

John dropped Oksana off at the gas station with several empty tanks and he and I drove over to the General Store. John crowbarred the door open. I knew I should have brought mine.

"Ok, load up honey, I'll stand watch," he said.

I grabbed as many perishable items as still seemed edible: some cheeses, some tortillas. I knew that soon I probably wouldn't be eating those things ever again, so now was the time. We grabbed all kinds of canned stuff and loaded it in the car. No zombies at all. I was kind of surprised. I grabbed a bottle of Jack Daniels for me and we shut the door the best we could and left.

"You don't get to keep the JD girly," John said. "We split everything."

We picked up Oksana who had 3 tanks of gas ready to go and headed back to the compound. This time there were many zombies on the road, as if they could sense we had been there and were waiting. We went around some, but there were so many we had to slow down, and we had to hit some.

Then the car stalled. Crap. Shivers went down my spine. It started up again right away, but there were tons of zombies on the car now.

"Go, GO!" Oksana yelled.

We took off, mowing them down, but several were still on the hood trying to smash the window. We finally shook them off. When we got to the compound, there were a ton of them at the gate. I was ready, jumped out of the car while it was still moving and started firing at them like Rambo. I fired and fired and fired and they kept going down.

Oksana yelled, "Nyet Esther, Stop!" and I did, but just as the last zombie fell to the ground.

I yelled, "Come on!" and went back to grab the goods out of the car.

Oksana and John just sort of stood there.

I said, "What?" and turned to look back at the gate and then I saw what I had done.

Brad was one of the figures lying motionless on the ground.

"Brad was just helping a new lady to get in safely." Oksana said as she and John frantically resumed grabbing stuff, nodding at the dead woman next to Brad. "That's why zombies were at gate, trying to get her. Next time, look at what you are doing."

We grabbed our stuff like lightning and ran in the gate, just as Brad and one other zombie were getting up. Oh God, I must not have hit them squarely in the head. We were too busy carrying goods to finish the job after the gate was closed. As we went up the causeway I looked back to see Brad lumber off into the woods.

I was in shock. I didn't know what to say or do. Can a day go by when I don't have a knot in my stomach with some new horror? I crawled into my bunk. Nobody bothered me or asked me to cook and clean like I was supposed to. Bridgett finally came by and I was crying.

"It's OK," she said, "We've all done it, we've all made mistakes, and we're all going through this nightmare together."

I told her about my family, about Tommy.

"I worry about Brenda too. She's my younger sister, and I don't want anything to happen to her. Unfortunately she is shy and doesn't do much around here, and she just watches what's going on without saying much."

I was only half-listening.

"I killed my friend today, Bridgett," I said, tears running down my face.

"I know," she said.

I can't write any more today.

Esther

DAY 7

After Bridgett left I eventually got up and did my cooking and cleaning chores. I powered through everything even though I was so numb. It would have been better if someone had have come to punish me or at least reprimand me, but no-one did. I shouldn't have bothered going to bed I was so upset, there was no way I could sleep. Oksana didn't stop by again. I think she's still mad at me.

I saw Brenda for the first time today. She was getting something from inventory. She looked at me squarely but didn't say anything, and then went upstairs. She looks a lot like Bridgett.

Speaking of which, Bridgett was kind to me earlier. She's a good friend. I laid there and for the first time I wished the moaning was louder, because no matter how loud it was I could still hear Jenny somewhere in the house alternating screaming and crying. It finally stopped, so I think someone gave her a sedative, or a lot of alcohol. All night long every time I heard a gunshot it reminded me of what I had done and I pictured Brad lying there and I heard Jenny screaming in my head. I never even got to hear what he had to say about what happened out front when we rescued Michael and Rose. I was in agony worse than I had previously felt, even with all that had happened.

I finally got up and went and quietly stole my bottle of Jack out of inventory and took my shotgun and climbed back in my bunk. I drank several shots worth out of the bottle and lay there with the shotgun under the covers lying on top of me with my finger on the trigger. With tears streaming down my cheeks I finally got enough nerve to pull the trigger, all the time thinking about poor Brad, and how stupid I had been, and how his girlfriend might feel. I lay there half-drunk just wanting it all to end. I have been through so much and I just killed a poor man, someone who is my friend. I decided to pull the trigger, to be free. I could just be free. Then all of a sudden it occurred to me that in order for Brad to have gotten up and walked away a zombie, he must have already had been bitten by one of them, before I shot him.

So that was it! I may have shot him, but he was already a zombie, or he was infected and on his way to becoming one, what's the difference? A wave of relief fell upon me and I slid the shotgun out of the covers and onto the floor. I then slept…some. I had still killed the lady whom I didn't know who had almost gotten to safety. I found out later her name was Zoe. Poor Zoe never had a chance. But then again, it seems most people aren't getting a chance.

In the morning John and I started teaching Michael and Rose how to shoot. John let me do a lot.

I told them, "This isn't something you *want* to do… it's something you *have* to do."

I taught them how to compensate for the wobbling the zombies do, to hit them in the head. Rose was a much better shot than Michael.

He was like, "I never thought in a million years that my wife could not only shoot a gun, but shoot people, and as well as she can!"

He was downright proud of her.

Rose just said, "I do it because I have to. I
do it because I have to."

She was like me when I started. I'm colder
now. Much colder. Living this life, it
hardens you, it hardens you and it's in your
best interest that it does. But I see how
Michael loves Rose. I see how Jack and
Oksana love each other. I want that. Do I
get to have a love life? Having this hard life
it seems there's no room for romance.

On our recon mission today, we took the
same car. Oksana went to the burned-down
rec center, attempting to hot-wire a Pine
Ridge patrol jeep. John and I went back to
the General Store. The store was quiet
again, and we could be quieter because we
didn't have to break in this time.

John said, "See Darlin', easy as pie."

On one of our trips to load the car, Oksana
drove up in one of the jeeps, waved, and
drove off, I assume back to the compound.
I felt for her driving on her own. Driving

even a mile in these conditions is a big deal, but it's better than walking!

On one of our trips loading the car, while I was getting canned goods in the back, John stepped over to me quietly with big eyes and I heard a loud snarl from behind him. He put his finger to his mouth to be quiet and I reached for the shotgun across my back in a sling. I looked behind him and saw the top of a head moving down the center aisle. We slowly backed into the bathroom across from the cold shelving section and shut the door quietly. My heart was racing. We sat there with both shotguns pointed towards the little door. We sat motionless for an hour, but nothing happened. Eventually we relaxed a little, but still didn't want to leave quite yet.

Then, and I will never forget this, John reached over and kissed me.

I said, "What are you doing?"

He coyly responded, "What ya think sexy, should we take advantage of the privacy and have a little lovin'?"

I very firmly said, "Hell no. We're not even out of this situation alive yet, I'm not…"

He cut me off. "Oh babe, I've wanted a piece of you since we met."

He put his weight on me, put one hand over my mouth and another holding my shotgun down. Then he started to try to get my pants undone. I kneed him where it hurts and shoved as hard as I could. He let out a yelp, and I got up without my shotgun, opened the door and ran. I got to the front door of the store and ran out, right into the zombie, who I think I actually surprised. She turned and hissed and started to grab me. I slammed her against the wall and continued to run.

I could hear John yelling, "I'll get you!" in the background, and the zombie groaning in pursuit of me also.

I ran and ran, wondering how I could make it back with the increase in zombie activity since I first was out here with Tommy, when Oksana drove by in the Jeep.

I frantically climbed in and said, "Go! John and a zombie are after me!"

She burned rubber and said, "John was bit?"

I told her no and explained while sobbing what happened on the way back to the compound.

We both went to see Jack. He was being consoled by another couple, Paul and Diana. I was so freaked out by what happened that I didn't bother to ask what was up for Jack. I re-explained what happened with John, and then to my surprise Oksana added to it.

"Yes. He tried to pull that sheet on me too, two week or so ago."

Jack was furious. "Well, then John gets what he gets. It's almost dark. I doubt he tries to come back here."

Of all the things that could happen to me, that's not something I thought would happen. I needed a friend, someone to talk to, and I wasn't sure about Oksana still, so I went to find Bridgett. She has always been there for me, always been so understanding. I searched the compound, but couldn't find her. I looked her up on the schedule board, and it said that she was still out getting firewood, her job. But she should have been back with her group hours ago. I went back to Jack.

"Where's Bridgett?" I demanded.

Paul spoke for Jack, who was still down and out. "We lost Bridgett today, Esther. She went for firewood and never came back."

"That doesn't mean she's *lost!*" I retorted. Crying, I ran upstairs to the east balcony to look down at the pile of bodies to be burned. She wasn't there. I ran to the west balcony where Michael and Rose were working as snipers.

Michael knew why I was there before I even asked.

"She's out there," he said. "We've been seeing her for a few hours now, but haven't tried to shoot her. She hasn't posed a threat."

I grabbed his binoculars and there she was,
wandering aimlessly around the west
quadrant, blood dripping from her mouth.

"Goodbye my friend. Thank you for being
there for me. I'm sorry I wasn't there for
you when you needed me to get your back."

I just stared. Poor Brenda.

God help us. God help us all.

Esther

DAY 8

Last night I retired to my new favorite
place. I found a trapdoor in the ceiling of a
closet upstairs that leads to the attic. I like it
because it's private and I can get in and out
without anybody noticing. I sat up there and
drank most of the rest of my bottle of Jack.
It helps me forget. I am a hollow shell of
the person I once was. I started making
friends with Rose, but I'm not getting too
close. I'm afraid I'll lose her. I am afraid of
making friends with anyone. I went back to
my bunk, still a little drunk, in the wee
hours so no-one would miss me at sun-up.

Oksana came by in the morning. "I am
sorry you lose good friend. I was starting to
know Bridgett my own self. I think if…"
and she was cut off by a new alarm I hadn't
heard before.

I think they've upgraded the system again.
So many people running around. We were
closer to the security camera station than
the front door, so we went there right away.
Brenda was already there, watching what
was going on, but as usual, wasn't saying

anything. I wonder how she is getting on after losing her sister.

We could see four people on the monitor running towards the gate at full tilt, and there were seven or so zombies after them, two only a few paces behind. It looked like a football game, except there was no football, and getting tackled meant death. In fact, that's exactly what happened to the person to the rear, who went down and was immediately enveloped by four of the zombies. That's not the way I want to go I tell you. I'd rather pop the pin of a grenade and hold it to my chest like Vasquez and Gorman from the movie *Aliens*.

At the front door, Patrol members Blake and Julie, in heavy riot gear, went out to the gate to help the three remaining runners. The door slammed behind them.

I hate that transition from inside the house to outside the gate. It's limbo: not quite safe, not quite in danger.

The gate was opened remotely and the first man made it inside, running past Blake and Julie to the front door. Brenda opened it for

him and left the door open and he ran in at
a hundred miles an hour. The second man
was tackled by a zombie as he went through
the gate. Blake grabbed him and pulled
while Julie went for her machete for close
quarters combat. The gate flew fully open.
She struck the zombie in the shoulder area
repeatedly, blood spraying, and finally
managed to cut his head off. He
immediately let go of the second person,
who was freaking out. Unhindered now, the
man got up and ran towards the front door,
escorted by Julie who collapsed in
exhaustion just inside the front door.

Meanwhile the third zombie was attacking
Blake from behind, who had dropped his
pistol while helping Julie. Blake shrieked.
The third man tried to pull the zombie off
of Blake but the zombie bit him and he fell
backwards. By this time, the four zombies
who got the first man were rushing the gate,
and they were joined by several others who
had come there because of the noise.

From inside the front door, Julie could see
that Blake was down with a zombie
practically on top of him, without his gun,
the third man was bitten and down,

becoming a zombie himself, and at least ten zombies rushing towards the fully open gate and Blake just inside.

"Blake!" Julie yelled from the floor.

"Shut the door!" Jack yelled. "There's nothing we can do for him. We've lost the gate."

Everyone just stared out the door at Blake down the corridor and the zombies about to envelope him inside the gate.

"SHUT the door, Brenda!" Jack yelled again.

Brenda reached out to the door, but instead of closing it, flung it fully open, and ran outside.

"Brenda!" Jack called out.

She ran full tilt at Blake, but the third man was now a zombie, and all of them were on him. Brenda flew into the lot of zombies, who were bunched together, sending most of them careening backwards out the gate, herself included.

Brenda was lying on the driveway dazed, but only for a second. She shook her head, got up and ran towards the gate, slamming it shut, behind her, reached down and grabbed Blake's pistol and fired into the back of the head of the zombie on top of Blake. The zombie slumped, and fell off of him.

Everyone just stared in shock for several seconds. There was Blake and Brenda standing inside the closed gate with a dead zombie at their feet.

"Yay!" everyone shouted.

Jack and several others went out to retrieve Blake and Brenda while the tackled zombies were just now getting up and grabbing the gate and hissing at them.

Everyone was still shouting and clapping for what Brenda had done. I was amazed at the entire incident. We could have lost Blake. We could have lost the gate all the way to the front door, but thanks to Brenda, we're OK!

"I owe you one," Blake told Brenda.

"It's something anyone here would have done for you, Blake," Brenda said back.

"Well that may be, but you saved my life anyway. Keep my gun, OK?"

Jack patted her on the head as she went by and said, "Good job Brenda. Good job in not doing what I said."

He was very pleased.

Wow what a day! Two men made it! I am happy when people make it here, but it's another mouth to feed. The first man's name was John I learned, a new John to replace the old one. I wonder what happened to him… the bastard! The second man who barely made it- his name was Rick. Everyone cleaned up and we could relax a little. What a joke. There's no such thing as relaxing around here. I did get a chance to talk to Rose. What a great person she is, and she always dresses so pretty, despite the circumstances.

I was starting to get ready to go on my recon mission for the day, when the alarm went off again. This time I went to the front door. At the front door, Patrol guys Rodney and Blake were bringing in someone. I had trouble seeing over the people.

It was John, the one who tried to rape me, and they weren't rescuing him, they were dragging him in.

Jack walked up from behind yelling, "Make a hole!" and people moved aside.

He walked right up to John, grabbed him by the collar, dragged him out the dining room French doors onto the back deck. He pulled out his 45 auto sidearm, and fired into the back of John's head. John slumped. Blood ran everywhere.

"Everyone!" Jack shouted. "This is what happens to people who fuck with the women. There is no second chance, there is no nothing. Take his boots and clothes off, and put them in inventory and burn his body," Jack instructed and walked away.

If he hadn't assumed leadership before, he had now.

I don't know if I can take so much

excitement, one thing happening after another. My heart was pounding!

I am not sure how much better I felt about the situation, but I did feel somewhat vindicated. I wonder how much this had to do with John being so stupid as to mess with Jack's woman, or if losing Bridgett the day before was a major factor. Jack was getting married tomorrow. I wonder.

My recon trip got canceled for the day. Jack gave me a new job. I am now in charge of all the recon missions, and Oksana has a new job too of some sort, so I get two new partners. He probably doesn't want his wife-to-be doing such a dangerous job. I am also taking over John's job of training people how to shoot, and I am no longer cooking and cleaning. I am glad. I was afraid they were going to make me clean up John's blood and brains on the deck.

I saw Brenda again today and I waved at her. She smiled at me and waved back. She was looking at the deck where John was killed. I figured she'd go back upstairs again, but instead she came over to me.

"Esther, I'm all alone without Bridgett. I hear you are giving the shotgun classes now. Can you show me? I think I want to get more involved. I also want to learn how to shoot this pistol."

"Sure Brenda," I said. "as long as it's OK with your dad."

"Yes, I already asked. He's fine with it."

She seems to have come out of her shell. I am very sad about Bridgett, but maybe I can become friends with Brenda, and watch out for her as Bridgett would have.

I took Brenda, John, and Rick up to see Michael and Rose. They were picking off zombies that were trying to get in. Michael was hitting every other one, Rose never missed.

"Brad is down there," Rose said without looking up.

"Thanks for reminding me." I said back.

It made me angry she said that, but I do know that it's hard to be a sniper as much as it's hard to do recon jobs. You do what you have to mentally too. Sometimes just venting is enough.

After they watched Michael and Rose a while I started to show them shotgun basics for themselves – how to aim and how to save your shells to be reloaded – when I heard screaming on the bottom floor of the house. It always scares me when stuff like this happens. What else can happen today? I didn't go see. Diana came up later to deliver coffee, and she knew what happened.

"We lost Julie," she said carefully, not knowing whether or not I was close to her.

"What happened?" I wanted more info.

"When she killed the zombie at the gate, she apparently got some zombie blood on her, and somehow or another, she got infected much later. She knew it was happening, and knew what Blake or Rodney would do to her any moment. Without hesitating, she opened the front door and gate and just ran out into the woods while she was still human."

Rick's head sunk. He knew what she did for him, what she sacrificed.

"Oh God," I said.

How terrible. I sipped my coffee and tried not to let it bother me, but it does. It eats at me. The longer I'm here the more I realize that sooner or later it will happen to all of us.

Esther

DAY 9

Today is the big day. I have been looking forward to it for a while now, and after today I will go back to not having something to look forward to. Sometimes it's the little things that keep us going.

I slept in a little for once, and had a cup of weak tea while watching everyone set up chairs on the back deck. Boy was it a mismatch of chairs too. My bunk is on the back deck so I could have watched the wedding in style if I wasn't the one officiating it. I couldn't help but notice John's blood was still there on the deck, just a stain now. What a sad reminder. Then I noticed the moaning around us, which normally I put out of my mind because I'm used to hearing it. Michael and Diana continued to work as snipers and our new John watched the security monitors while everyone else attended the wedding.

Between occasional gunshots, the moaning, and all the people dressed in whatever they happened to own for the wedding, it was quite the bizarre scene.

Jack went up to the front and I went to meet him. He was giddy. People finally seemed to sit down and Rose started to try to play the wedding march on a bass guitar. I laughed under my breath. I guess it's the closest thing to an organ we had. Then, Oksana appeared at the back. She looked beautiful with her long black hair flowing down her chest and a white dress of some sort that was clearly way too big for her. I could see her black combat boots sticking out from underneath the dress. How funny.

Jack was nervous.

"Three time's the charm," he said

Oksana started to walk down the aisle with Paul holding her arm. I started thinking about the lines I was supposed to recite again when I started noticing that the frequency of gunshots was increasing. Jack also noticed and looked at me momentarily. The moaning was getting loader too. Oksana arrived at the front and Jack took her hand.

I made a conscious decision days ago not to mention the conditions we were under in my little speech. I felt that people would rather hear something normal for once – something to relate to – like comfort food.

"Dearly beloved, we are gathered here today to join two people in holy matrimony."

I mistook Jack's nervousness for pre-wedding jitters. Jack interrupted me, looked into Oksana's eyes, and hurriedly said the following, if I remember it right:

Oksana, you are the best thing that's ever happened to me. You are kind, loving, and incredibly gorgeous. You are capable, cultured, intelligent and wise. I would be so lucky to be your husband, no matter how long or how short our time is together. In these desperate times, I promise to be there for you when you need me, not only in surviving this insanity around us, but for the little things too. I promise to be faithful, loyal, and deserving of your respect.

Right about then I noticed John in the background, near the security monitors, waving his arms in the air to get our attention.

Then there was a *lot* of banging on the
north wall.

Oksana opened her mouth to say her vows,
but instead looked at me with pleading eyes
and simply said, "Marry us....*now.*"

"I now pronounce you man and wife."

Jack reached over and kissed her
passionately. It was such a happy moment,
that briefly took away so much of the hurt I
had been feeling, but intuitively I still knew
something was very wrong, and they did
too. A moment later, our world would go to
Hell, as it has so many times before,
throwing me into utter darkness and
despair.

As we all stood there in shock, the entire
north wall came crashing down inward,
covered in zombies. We weren't prepared.
We got lazy.

It was utter chaos, people firing guns in
close quarters, lots of friendly fire. It was
insane. I heard Rose yell "Help me!" She
didn't even have a chance. I turned to see
them pull her arm off and she was swept

away in an instant. Jack and Oksana ran to
get weapons, but one of the zombies turned
and grabbed Oksana's long hair. They
pulled her down and were on top of her,
and I didn't see anything more as I ran
myself to get a gun, to get *anything*, and get
away from them.

Paul, who was near Oksana the entire time
was already a zombie, snarling into the air
like a Werewolf, and going after others.
When Michael saw that they got to Rose, he
just started screaming and firing inside the
compound at anything that looked zombie-
like, and shot at least two of our people in
the process. I ran towards my bunk to get
my shotgun but there was a zombie there. I
ran to the security station, but there was a
zombie there that John was fighting off. I
ran to the west wall and I was blocked off
from the rest of the compound by three of
them.

I screamed, "Come get me mother f-ers!"

and without looking slammed into the first
one that came after me, pushing us both
into some wedding chairs. I went to get up

and I saw it was Bridgett. My heart stopped.
I got up but she had me by my hair too.

I yelled, "No Bridgett!" and pulled hard,
and I swear, half of my hair came out.

She then got my leg and I pulled it away but
she scratched me really hard. I yelped but
jerked myself up and forward. Another
zombie pawed at my legs again, but I had
the strength to push forward again, and I
looked for an exit – I had no choice.

I ran for the north side, ran over the
downed wall and leaped over the side, and
down to the ground. There were zombies all
around me but most of them were
concentrating on getting inside the
compound. I ran into the woods. I could
hear shotguns in the background going off
like crazy. No-one followed me.

I am alone again in the woods. I am alone
and I have abandoned the only place that
has kept me safe and the only people that
have kept me alive for over a week now. I
abandoned them.

I am alone, and I think I am dying.

Esther

DAY 10

Well, I am alive. I am human still, but whatever I have, I am sick.

I spent the night in a small enclave with a little opening down by a creek in the wash. I could hear gunshots all night and some moaning around me. I didn't sleep much, but I catnapped. It's cold this time of year. I am so sick. I looked down and my leg was more like clawed than scraped. There are pieces of Bridgett's fingernails in the cuts. This scrape is really bad and I'm really sick but I'm not a zombie, so… what gives? I shivered. I can't believe it. I can't believe any of it. I don't know what to think.

I lay low for a long time trying to figure out what to do. I was too sick to really do any serious traveling, and where would I go? Back to the compound? Is it taken? Is everybody dead? Can I expect to see everyone I have lived with wandering around the woods looking to eat me?

I lay there and listened to the shots being fired to see if I could make any sense of it. Then the shotguns stopped. This scared me badly, but then, then I heard….what…seemed to be guns, but not the same guns, like rifles. We had hardly any rifles. We put scopes on our shotguns because we could use them to see like binoculars, not because they had a long range.

Then I heard what really sounded like a rifle.

I got up and put weight on my leg. Actually it wasn't too bad, just hurt. I hurt everywhere. My heart hurt the most. What a thing to have happen on their wedding. I wonder if they are OK? I crept along the creek so that my noise would be drowned out, and followed it up to the general location where the compound was, to get a better view. When I got there, I could see that there were zombies surrounding the place, but the north wall was up again. That was a good sign – sort of surprised me. I considered having a closer look.

There, that was definitely a rifle going off. It all of a sudden occurred to me that somebody might try to shoot me, especially after yesterday's free-for-all, so I left the wash and went up onto the town streets.

There was a lot of carnage near the compound. Besides the zombie bodies, there were a lot of human bodies strewn about also. I'm guessing the reason there weren't more bodies lying around is because they're now zombies too. I don't know why some people die and stay dead and others become zombies. I was stepping over people, some of which I knew, and then I saw a smaller body lying in a heap face down and sprawled out. It was Brenda, still with Blake's pistol in her hand. With tears streaming down my face I reached down and straightened her little body up and patted her head.

"It's going to be OK now honey. It's all OK now."

I took the gun and put it in my waistband. Poor Brenda. I swallowed hard, put it out of my mind, and moved on.

It took me a while to get to the front area, and it was quite different than usual. There were military jeeps in the street! Forgetting for a moment that I sort of abandoned them, I went up to the gate and banged.

"Please let me in, I'm Esther, and I need help."

I could hear the automated speakers playing Oksana's voice "Do not behave erratically. Do not make noise, or you will be shot." I was hoping to hear her real voice, and be let in.

Instead, I heard a man's voice I didn't know. "Esther, advise us if you have any injuries."

I told him I did but that I wasn't infected.

"We'll be the judge of that. I'll let you in but you have to talk to the lieutenant."

 Lieutenant? I didn't know what to think, but when he buzzed me in, I was happy just to have chain-link fence between me and the zombies.

When I got to the front door, there was a big metal camouflage phone hanging on the wall next to the door, which wasn't there before. I didn't have to knock. I picked it up and heard the man from before. "Ok, we'll let you in," he said and the door opened.

The whole thing was so odd. It's like I had been gone a week! Two men in cammo met me at the door. This is Sergeant Campbell and I'm Lieutenant Johnson.

"I'm pleased to meet you." I shook their hands.

Campbell spoke. "We arrived last night a while after you guys were attacked, and helped get things under control. If I had to guess, I'd say we arrived just in time."

"Great," I said. I really wasn't sure what to make of these guys so I made sure to act like I thought them being there was the best thing since fried cheese.

"Can I speak to Jack or Oksana?"

They took me to Jack. I was straight with him. "Talk to me."

He looked up at me with wet eyes and I knew.

"My Oksana's gone. My Brenda's gone."

He covered his face with his hands and wept.

I knew how he felt. He was crying for Oksana, Brenda, and Bridgett still too, I'm sure. How horrible to lose your wife and children all in a matter of a couple of days. I didn't tell him about Bridgett attacking me. Either he knew or he didn't, but it wasn't going to help anything.

"Jack, I am so sorry, but we need to regroup, we need to deal with it and survive."

Words I scarcely believe could come out of my mouth.

"Tell me who else. Who else did we lose?"

"Rose. We lost Rose. Michael went nuts. Michael killed Rick by accident. We lost Paul. We lost John. We lost others you don't know."

Sergeant Campbell was standing nearby and stepped into the conversation. "We're giving you supplies: rifles, ammo, mortars, grenades, food, medical supplies, and assorted other stuff."

Jack explained later what a mortar was. Sadly, the biggest thing I was interested in getting was a grenade - for a last minute way out for me.

Campbell continued, "We want to see if there's anyone else still alive out there, so we're moving on tomorrow."

Lieutenant Johnson said, "If you think you're OK, let's take a look at that leg of yours in the morning. Until then, get some rest."

I gave Jack a hug, and followed Johnson out to the back. On the way I heard Michael somewhere yelling.

"She was good woman, she was a good shot. Now you expect me to get on that damn balcony and shoot at her? Don't you get it, she was my wife! I won't do it! I won't do it I tell you!"

I don't know who he was talking to, but I didn't blame him. I missed Rose.

As soon as I got to the deck I looked around to make sure it was safe. It was so creepy to look at where we had spent so much time and now I could see where Oksana was taken and Rose, and I didn't want to think about it.

I got in my bunk and after a few moments of thinking, pulled out my knife and cut my hair off. Never again would I give a zombie something to grab onto. I didn't get enough showers anyway, and who do I need to impress? *I still have my red nails*, I thought to myself, chipped as they are. I don't have to look completely like a boy.

Of course, right after that, Sergeant Campbell came to the back deck with the new guy Johnson and another new guy – his name is Dale I found out later, and he's a Private– bringing supplies with them. Wow, is he cute! I only saw him for a moment but I am all of a sudden feeling like I should have kept my hair. I don't know why I'm feeling this. Forget it. He'll just die like all the rest.

I crawled under the covers, thinking I would consider all that had happened and weep, but I was sick and exhausted, and quickly fell asleep. The last thing I saw before drifting off was Michael on the west balcony... shooting at zombies.

Esther

DAY 11

I lay in my bunk on that quiet-for-once night on my side, looking out over the deck. Two of the 55 gallon drums were still burning, and one had gone out already. Nobody was standing around them keeping warm at this late hour. I was numb. So much had gone on in the past day- I was playing it over in my mind. I didn't notice the figure below me until it was too late.

Slowly, a head rose to my bunk level. It was Bridgett! She grabbed me and held me down and starting biting me and ripping large chunks of flesh off my arm.

Oh God. I sat up. What a terrible dream. I lay there, shaking. I missed Bridgett. This world is so upside down. Finally I got up, but I was still sick. I didn't care. I had finished my bottle of Jack, and went to steal another. I went into the garage quietly and listened for anyone before turning the light on. I turned it on and there was Michael, holding a bottle of Peppermint Schnapps. He wouldn't look at me and finally said something.

"I….came down here to get a blanket out of inventory - I have authorization I swear - and I ….I saw this and I …."

I could already smell alcohol on his breath.

"It's OK," I told him, "I understand."

He nodded, hid the bottle under his coat while still looking down and disappeared up the stairs. I returned to my own mission. Ironically, we were both there for the same reason. There was no more Jack. I looked at what was there and grabbed the bottle of Barcardi 151. I snuck up into the attic and drank myself into oblivion.

I used to think about what would cause this virus, or whatever it is. I used to consider what it meant to be civilized. Humans are just a more civilized form of animal. Maybe evolution is correcting an error? Maybe we were always supposed to be just dumb, instinctual, animals. I don't think about that stuff much anymore. I think about my family sometimes, but not as much as I used to. I think about practicing shooting. I think about lifting weights. I think about how to stay quiet. I think about going to the attic and drinking.

Near dawn in my stupor, I could hear the alarm system go off way below me. I tried to tell if it was an alert for humans arriving – or zombies arriving. I didn't care. I passed out again.

When I finally sobered up it was almost 10 in the morning. I snuck out of the attic and back downstairs into the bustle of people working and the military getting ready to leave.

Jack found me. He was not happy.

"Nice hair. What happened to our recon mission today, Esther?" he queried.

I played the victim card.

"Jack, I had a rough night, I lost a lot of friends."

He looked down and said, "Me too," patted me on the back, and walked away.

The pain he was clearly holding back was formidable.

On his way out he turned back around and said, "That won't work tomorrow you know."

He faked a smile and walked on. I should have played the still sick card.

Oh my gosh! I had forgotten to see what the alarm was about. Obviously it wasn't a zombie attack. Two new people arrived: Tonya and Rhonda. They were both crying. The military was questioning them. All of a sudden I got a weird feeling. They're supposed to leave today. Why haven't they left yet? Why do I feel this way, we need all the help we can get? I don't know. I like Private Dale. The rest of them I don't really care about.

I took Tonya and Rhonda to get some supplies, to find a place to sleep, and then of course, up to the west balcony for sniper practice. They both seem nice. Rhonda might make a good cook. Tonya, on the other hand, might be a good person to go on recon missions. They were thinking

about surviving. I had bigger plans for
them.

The military was packing up. I watched
them drive off from the east balcony. I was
ambivalent. The good news is Private Dale
and Lieutenant Johnson stayed behind.
Johnson is an OK guy, but I'm really happy
Dale is staying.

When I took Tonya and Rhonda to the west
balcony, Michael wasn't there. Diana was
firing at some zombies that were trying to
get in, all by herself.

"Where's Michael?" I asked.

"I don't know, but I could sure use the
backup. I swear there are more of them
every day."

 I looked at her and thought about Paul.
She's handling it pretty well. I knew Michael
wasn't. He had scrawled something on the
west wall I didn't really look at. Spray
painting as a form of venting on the back
deck walls was something people had been
doing since before I got there. One of

things someone wrote was "*All Hope is Gone*". That one stuck with me.

I still wondered where Michael might be. I had an idea. "Ladies, I'll be right back."

I went down into the garage. He wasn't there. Then I noticed a foot sticking out from behind one of the crates. I went around the corner and there was Michael, sitting on the floor, several empty bottles around him, holding a shotgun to his chin and visibly shaking.

"I can't do it anymore, Esther, I can't. I miss her, I love her. I can't shoot at those things knowing my wife is out there and I might have to shoot her too."

"Michael, I know how hard this has been for you. I once put my shotgun to my head too, after I accidentally killed Brad. Do you remember him? He helped you in when you got here. I understand how you feel about Rose, and about killing Rick too."

"I didn't kill Rick, I shot him, but he was already a zombie."

I didn't know that.

"Michael, when you were down here last, I was getting a bottle too, OK? I have a lot of pain I'm dealing with anyway I can too."

"I just can't shoot at zombies, knowing Rose is out there."

"Michael, it's going to be OK, we'll get you another job, OK? I know they'll do that for you."

"No they won't, I already asked. Jack says I'm too experienced. It won't help anyway. If somebody else is shooting up there I'll think of her every time I hear a gunshot."

Michael closed his eyes. "Tell everyone I said goodbye. Tell them I'm sorry."

Then he pulled the trigger.

Esther

DAY 12

I'm feeling better, which is a very good thing. My leg has healed. So apparently, scratches or no scratches, I wasn't infected. A lot happened today, so I have a lot to write about.

Last night I thought a lot about Michael. I've seen enough brains blown out of people's heads by now not to be bothered by that…but he really took losing his wife hard. I get it - he felt he couldn't bear another day without her. *That's really something* I thought as I snuck down to inventory to get a bottle of booze. Half of Michael was still there. I stared for a while at the mess, and looked over the bottles of alcohol. I kept thinking about him and I thought of how much easier it was for him than for Rose, or Oksana, or anybody who was eaten or mauled into a zombie. I grabbed a bottle of bourbon. Then I walked over to the ammo crates and stared at them for a while, while drinking right out the bottle, in the open. I finally picked out a grenade, hid it under my shirt, and went upstairs. Someday it might come in handy. I'd rather have a way out if the time comes

and I'm surrounded. I'd rather have a way
out if I felt like Michael did.

For some reason it then sunk in that
Michael was really gone. *Oh God, Michael!*

I needed to calm down. Why do I keep
saying that? "Oh God." So many prayers
were falling on deaf ears. So much pain and
suffering.

I slept… some. I awoke to smelling
something terrible from the kitchen and
wondered if it was Rhonda's cooking. I was
considering skipping breakfast when I saw
that Blake and Dale were making some sort
of acid to drop on zombies in the sink. So
THAT'S what stunk. I stopped by to say hi
to them both. Blake smiled at me and
looked at Dale and said "I need to use the
bathroom, I'll be back". I was sort of happy
to be alone with Dale.

"Can I help you with that?" I asked him.

He said, "Sure, I need a test subject. Put
your head in the sink and we'll see how
good this acid is".

"No way!" I recoiled.

Dale changed the subject. "So I heard you know how to shoot really well."

"Well I, no not really." I countered.

"Well you sure seem to be kicking ass around here in my book. You civis need leaders. That's pretty cool you're helping like that."

It was great to hear someone talk nicely about me, especially Dale. It made me smile. Then I remembered… then I remembered what happened to Rose – what happened to Michael, what happens to everybody…

I'll see you later." I stuttered and walked away briskly.

"Hey, you want to hang out later?" Dale called out to me as I went outside towards my bunk.

I didn't answer him. I can't. I just can't.

I got ready for my recon mission with my new partner, Diana. Tonya's too green, so it's just the two of us today. Diana's a good shot, but not as good as Rose…nobody was as good as Rose, but a good shot none-the-less. Tonya stayed behind and learned to shoot with Johnson, who replaced Michael as a sniper.

We had to walk today. Unfortunately there weren't any vehicles for us to take. Sure, plenty of cars were sitting around, but we'd either driven them until they ran out of gas or siphoned the gas already. The close ones I mean. Maybe someday we'll go on a gas hunting mission, but we'll need a car to carry the gas back.

Our mission was to go to several houses nearby that were known to have equipment we might use. We hiked up a hiking trail rather than up Main Street to one such house, a house that had a welding unit in it. We were supposed to confirm it was there and bring back any accessories, and the military twosome, as we called them-Johnson and Dale- would get the actual welder later. We went quietly along the ground, from tree to tree, shotguns in hand. We passed by some zombies undetected.

Diana wanted to shoot them. This was not a good idea. I kept thinking about Dale.

As we went east towards the end of the residential street near the top of the canyon, we walked by a house that intrigued me. Ok it scared me. There were little bloody handprints about two feet off the ground on the front door, side door, and garage door. I had never seen a zombie child before other than my own brother Tommy, and that was before I knew what they were. I had to check it out. We opened the front door, which was unlocked, and covered each other as we slowly went in. There weren't any handprints anywhere, but I was scared to death anyway. There's something about little munchkins running around trying to eat you that is utterly unnerving. We went into each room and saw nothing. Clearly this place was an after-school daycare back in the Real World. There were children's playthings everywhere: dolls, stuffed animals, toys. Then I heard a noise and couldn't tell where it was coming from. It sounded like banging of some kind. Diana found a locked bathroom door. There was no banging but a funny sound was coming out of it anyway.

We poked at the door, and nothing happened. I pulled out my trusty screwdriver and popped the pins out of the hinges. Then we pushed the door open the wrong way, just a little.

All I saw was a flash. Something was on me. I shrieked and fell backward and then I could see two zombie toddlers were on top of me. I threw one off and BANG, Diana shot it. The other one was trying to bite me but she was so small I knocked her over and got up and ran out the door. Diana was blowing away drywall behind me as I ran down the hall but the damn thing was still after me. I turned to see it but it was so small I couldn't. I ran into the kitchen and leaped up on the kitchen counter. I looked around. It was gone. My heart was pounding. Then I heard a squeak below me and a few feet over and I saw it had brought down the oven door and was standing on it, and was half-way onto the counter when BOOM, Diana blew it over the counter and though the kitchen window.

I was panting, but we needed to act fast: the noise would attract more zombies.

We continued our search of the house. I could still hear banging. I was creeped out at this point. I opened another bedroom door and there was another zombie child sitting on the bed. I raised my shotgun and then realized it wasn't a zombie, it was a malnourished human girl. I pointed around the rest of the room with my shotgun with my eyes where the shotgun pointed and talked at the same time.

"Can you talk?" I asked.

The girl said "Yes, I can talk."

I said "Are we safe in this room?"

"Safe from what?"

"Zombies!"

She said, "What are zombies?"

I lowered my gun.

Diana came into the room. "What's your name little girl?"

She said, "My name's Jolene. Where's my mommy?"

"How old are you?" I continued without answering.

"I'm eight and a half."

"Jolene, we need to go now, it's not safe. Do you have any other family members here?"

"The other kids' parents were supposed to pick them up, but Mommy locked them in the bathroom. I don't have any brothers or sisters. It's just Mommy and me, but I don't know where she went."

"How long ago was that?" I asked.

"I dunno, maybe, two weeks ago?" she said after thinking hard about it.

I was still shocked to find her. "Have you eaten, honey?"

"There is some food for us in the pantry. I eat candy and macaroni and the cheese packets and graham crackers and other stuff. Most of what was in the refrigerator went bad already."

We finished checking the rest of the house and were about to go outside again when Diana said "We should check the garage."

Diana stayed with Jolene and I went to the garage. The door to the garage had no threshold on the bottom and I could see sunlight coming through underneath it. I could see shadows. I could see movement. I opened the door and a middle-aged woman zombie stood there, blood dripping from her mouth. There were children's bodies everywhere, chewed up and bloody, and definitely not moving. I fired point blank and killed it.

Diana yelled, "You OK?"

I said, "Yep. I think I found what was making the banging."

My heart sank. Poor Jolene. I left and locked the door.

I told Jolene, "Sorry about making all the noise. We need to go now."

She said "I'm not going with strangers without my mommy!"

I told her that her mother had gone away and she would want her to go with us. What else do I say?

We confirmed the welder was at the house next door, didn't end up actually taking anything, and hurried back to the compound. We had taken on four new people while we were gone. Sheesh, where do they keep coming from?

I took Jolene to Jack and he was concerned.

"We have a hard enough time taking care of adults who can in fact take care of themselves. Who's gonna take care of this little girl?"

"I will!" I offered without thinking about it.

Jolene looked up at me and said, "Is Mommy in heaven?"

I didn't know what to say, because zombies don't fit real well into anything we've all been told as children. Frankly, I had Hell in mind.

"Yes dear, she's in heaven. She loves you very much and wants you to be OK and stay with me."

She started to whimper but was coping surprisingly well considering the circumstances.

I didn't realize it at the time, but Jolene was my salvation. That night, I put the grenade back. A tiny ray of hope had found a small chink in my armor.

Esther

DAY 13

Jolene slept in my bunk with me. I slept like
a baby. I got up early to catch some of
Rhonda's good cooking. There was actually
a line to get grub. What a difference from
the acid making smell yesterday! It reminded
me of Dale and I wondered where he was,
when he walked up from behind me.

"Hey, um, Esther, can we talk?"

Dale fumbled a bit. I wanted to talk to him,
but I didn't know how.

"OK," I fumbled back.

"Listen, I see you around, and well, I notice
how different you are from the other ladies.
You take charge, and I like that."

"…and I'm the only girl that's under 30
here too, right?" I blurted out for some
reason.

"Yes, and you're the most beautiful." Dale
looked down.

For some reason, that got me, just for a moment. Just for a moment I let the real world come back and let this young man touch my heart. But then it was gone as fast as it came, and reality came rushing back.

"Hey why don't you go find your better-half, Mr. Military Twosome?" I sort of threw this at him without looking as I got out of line and went out back.

Screw this.

Jack was standing by a drum on fire, drinking some coffee and keeping warm, when Diana yelled down from the balcony, "Hey Jack, your ex-wife is in front, trying to get in."

"Don't let her in," He yelled up to her.

"She's not a zombie," Diana yelled back.

"Wait... longer..." He laughed.

I walked back to my bunk where Jolene was still sleeping, and then I saw it. I don't know why I didn't see it before. There on the back deck wall right in front of me, was what Michael had written, which I hadn't really looked at. It said,

> *Yesterday my wife killed a zombie.*
> *Today she became one.*
> *Tomorrow I will have to kill her.*
> *Soon I may kill myself.*

I just stared at it. How can we go on? How can we cope? I wanted to go drink, but I had Jolene and other really important things to do.

No recon mission, I had a lot of new people to train today. I carried Jolene in my arms, wrapped in my sleeping bag.

I looked into the faces of the new recruits, each of them. I knew that the chances of all of them making it for long were not high. I looked at their physique. I looked into their eyes and tried to figure out their mental attitude. That's what counted the most. But in the end, none of it really matters. It's how long you're exposed to the threat that determines how long you live. As I've often remembered from the movie Fight Club, "On a long enough timeline *everyone's* survival rate drops to zero." Then I wondered if someday we'd be shooting *at them*. The chances were actually quite high.

Jack made me the number two person in charge of this place today. I was proud of myself. I can't believe that I'm 16 and these people are counting on me to keep them safe.

Lot of good it will do, I thought to myself.

I was showing the new recruits shotgun and rifle basics, when Jack came up. He saw Jolene sleeping and asked why I wasn't teaching her too.

"Because she's *eight*," I said, surprised.

"She's not going to school ever again Esther. She's not going to cheerlead, she's not going to get a degree. This is what she needs to learn right now, Esther. This is it."

I woke up Jolene and gave her an unloaded shotgun to play with.

"I point it at the zombies, right?" she asked. "Where's my bullets?"

"They're called 'shells' and you'll get them soon enough, dear."

I changed my focus to sniping. There was an unusually high amount of activity outside today, lots of zombies to shoot at for practice. *That's odd*, I thought. Then I heard Blake yelling at the security monitoring station downstairs. I stopped cold in my tracks. I stopped teaching. I stopped doing *anything*. It was like people around me and things occurring were in slow motion. I looked at the zombies banging on the walls. I looked down to see Blake pointing at the monitor and waving his arms. I assessed the situation so fast that I knew exactly what was happening before anyone else did. I recognized this feeling from the wedding. It was happening again.

No!

I grabbed and threw boxes of shells at the new recruits and yelled, "Kill them all!" while scooping up Jolene and running to the stairs.

I ran downstairs to my bunk and threw her in there and told her to stay low. I slung my shotgun, grabbed my knife, screwdriver, and several boxes of ammo and ran over to Blake.

"Where are they?"

He looked at me with a blank stare like he didn't know what to do.

"Where are they, Blake?" I repeated.

Finally he spoke. "We… lost the front gate."

I looked on the monitor and zombies had clawed their way through the gate and were pouring in and heading towards the front door.

"Blake, get the guys, barricade the front door."

From thirty feet away I could hear the first pounding on the front door. We were three inches away from being overrun. Johnson was firing a semi-auto rifle from the balcony into the causeway.

I heard Jack yell, "Reclaim the gate!"

Johnson threw a grenade in the causeway. There was a loud BANG sound and there were zombie body parts everywhere. When I could finally see after the dust cleared, they were pouring in again.

I looked up and Johnson was getting another grenade. I knew he had to be careful not to blow away our outer defenses and let more of them in. Jolene was up there with him.

"Jolene, what are you doing?" I yelled.

"Helping!" she said and I saw that she was throwing pieces of firewood down into the causeway onto the zombies' heads.

The banging on the front door was getting worse. They were getting through.

"We need help, and we need help now!" I yelled.

Jack stopped yelling commands briefly to others and said, "Esther – go find the military. Get them back here. They were stopping in the town at the base of the mountain, and should still be there."

I knew the town he was talking about. I
didn't hesitate. I ran to the kitchen to get
some provisions, trying to figure out how I
was going to leave the house since we
always went out the front door and gate.

Dale caught up with me. "We'll go, Blake
and I. We'll go find them."

"No!" I said. "Don't go."

He said nothing and looked at me. What
am I doing?

"Please stay with me."

These were MY words coming out of MY
mouth. He was still looking at me. He
reached out his hand and held mine, then
reached over and gently kissed me.
Electricity ran down my spine. I just stood
there, oblivious to everything around me.

"I have to go" I think he said. My head was
still spinning. I was about to argue again
when he looked at Jolene, running to get
more firewood.

He pointed at her and added, "She needs you. Stay with her, I'll go. It will be fine."

Johnson ran up to us at that moment. "Private Dale, Blake and I are going to regroup with the unit. You stay here."

A moment later, Johnson and Blake were out the second story window, dropped to the ground and were gone. Johnson was Dale's superior. I started to say how relieved I was when the next thing I know Dale is kissing me again. I forgot about everything, and kissed him back.

The screams I heard next brought me back to reality. The front door was folding inward. I could see zombie hands on the inside of the door at times, clawing to get in.

The "in charge" mode I was supposed to be in kicked in again. I gave Dale a big hug and ran upstairs and got several of the new recruits and told them what to do.

"You guys, fire at the front door at anything that moves."

Jack ran up with some boards and started boarding up the front door, in some cases nailing boards through zombie hands. Fortunately, the new recruits knew to stop firing. Rhonda and John were helping. Jenny was yelling "Screw you, you ugly sons of bitches!"

I ran upstairs to find Jolene. Diana followed me. I heard a smashing below. The front door caved. They were in. I heard Jack scream and then he was gone. I heard all kinds of screaming, coming from everywhere downstairs. Tonya was dragging a plywood board down the stairs to block it off as I was running upstairs.

Rhonda was trying to get through when he sealed her off. Behind the board I could hear her yelling, "For God's sake, don't leave me down here!"

I couldn't believe we were shutting out all those people, but I didn't know what to do either. I ran to Jolene and said, "Stay low sweetheart, I'll be back."

I ran back down to help with boarding up the stair-well. All I could hear other than

rifle and shotgun blasts was Rhonda
screaming to be let in, which stopped
presently.

Most of the people who made it upstairs
were new. I had no idea where Dale was.
Johnson and Blake were gone getting the
military. What were we going to do?

I ran to the west balcony and looked down.
The entire back deck was full of zombies.

Oh my God. We lost the entire bottom half
of the compound.

Esther

DAY 14

No sleep. Not much food. We are upstairs, boarding up the staircase to the second floor more and more with anything we can find. As far as I know, everyone that was downstairs when I went upstairs is dead…or worse. I turned at some point to see John walk towards me. I thought he was a zombie! The air was full of gun smoke. I almost shot him.

"How did you escape from downstairs?" I yelled over at him while still firing.

"I ran out on the deck and had a few seconds with no zombies around me to climb up a wall at a corner, to get to the balcony."

I was happy he made it. "I hope the zombies can't do that," I told him.

"Yeah me too," he remarked. "But it's just me. Someone behind me was trying to follow me up but they pulled him back down."

Tonya walked up. "You should see who's downstairs."

I went to the balcony, and it was unbelievable. Wandering around the back deck were many people I recognized, including Brad, Rick, John, Julie, Jack, and Oksana. Then I saw him. Oh my God my father was down there too! I closed my eyes. It was so horrible. I couldn't even think about it. I had to concentrate on Jolene.

I tried to figure out how we could retake the downstairs. We needed to act fast. We would run out of food and ammo up here soon, as all our supplies were stored downstairs. I was just thinking about Johnson and Blake bringing back the military when I heard the security station radios below squawking.

"Base, recon1, Come In."

I wish I had some way of getting a radio myself. The moaning *that close* was deafening, and I could barely hear what they were saying. I leaned way over the railing to hear.

"Shut up dammit!" I yelled in vain at the zombies moaning below.

"Base, recon1, Come In."

I was afraid they would stop trying and we'd never get an update. Then they finally just blurted it out.

"Base, we found the military. We found their jeeps crashed and on fire. There's no one alive. The entire military unit has been completely wiped out. I repeat. The military is completely wiped out. We're coming back to assist in reclaiming the front gate. We'll be back tomorrow."

Johnson was alive at least, and he didn't say anything about losing Blake. That's great, but we have lost the resources of the military and we can't even tell Blake and Johnson we've been overrun at the front door. At this point, all hope that I had of us surviving was gone. I had to tell Dale, but where is he?

I looked down again and a large portion of zombies were vacating the back deck. A moment later, I knew why.

Diana was yelling, "Get down here, they're getting through the barricade."

As I looked down, Dale was there, pushing with all his weight against the barricade. I tried to reinforce it with wood. I could hear John and others pounding zombies with their guns from the balcony. The zombies were pushing harder to get in. I ran to get them. Right now it was more important to keep zombies from coming up the stairs than just killing them on the back deck which we had already lost.

On my way back to the stairs, the barricade gave way. I didn't even see Dale go. He just wasn't there anymore, and I knew what happened. I fell to my knees. I never got to enjoy a relationship, I never got to feel alive, and now he's dead. I never even got to say goodbye.

Tears were pouring down my cheeks but I knew I had to keep it together. I couldn't do anything, I just lay there. I watched Jenny run up the stairs but she were pulled back down. Other people went soon after. I did nothing to help.

Finally I came to my senses and got up just in time to avoid zombies myself. Tonya ran one way, Diana another. I ran to find Jolene. I couldn't find her. I looked in the guest bedrooms, she wasn't there.

Then I heard her call out to me, "Esther!"

I turned to see her in the master bedroom through the master bedroom door. She ran into the master bathroom. Oh God! Zombies ran in after her. Jolene! I had no choice but to step inside the guest bedroom and close the door. I kicked myself for shutting that door, but what could I do? I heard Diana scream. I ran into the closet and closed the door, and then up into my familiar attic, through the trap door I had climbed so many times before. I closed the trap door. I heard John scream. All I heard was screaming all around me. I waited to hear something more.

Eventually the screaming died down and all I could hear below me was moaning, that damn constant moaning.

I wish I had that grenade.

Esther

DAY 15

I am all alone in this attic. I am all alone in this house.

I can hear a few shotgun blasts and yelling out front, which I am hoping is someone, *anyone*, surviving. I tried to poke a hole through the roof to look outside but the wood is too thick. I thought at first maybe they were people coming for me, coming to rescue me, but no one has.

I have no way of knowing if Blake and Johnson had any chance…any chance of making it back… any chance of surviving once they did.

I have no food, but I dare not leave this attic or even make a sound, in fear of alerting the zombies I'm up here.

The compound is lost, of that I am now certain. I can hear them below me, roaming the halls of a place I once called home for some time now. I was foolish to think we

had a chance. Humanity I mean. It's all gone
so terribly wrong.

My God, has it come to this? Shall I die of
starvation? Is that how this madness ends
for me? Is this the only reward for my
efforts - avoiding being infected by
those…creatures…who were once my
family, my friends, my neighbors, to
ultimately die alone in this forsaken attic of
starvation?

Tommy! Jolene! Dale! I picture them in
their final moments of life.

Sometimes I think I can tell which zombie
used to be someone I knew by their voice –
through all that *incessant* moaning. It's
insanity. The world has surely come to an
end. If I die here, know that I died trying.
Know that though the world has gone to
Hell and God has fled, that if someone *who
can still read*, reads this – know this – I was a
good person. I lived, I laughed, I loved, if
ever so briefly.

It ends soon for me, I know it. Please bury
me in the garden behind our house so that I
have some sort of dignity in death.

Esther Allison Timee

DAY 19

It's been several days since the bad attack. I
hid under the bathroom sink like Esther
taught me. I thought the zombies would eat
me, but they never found me. Two days ago
I sneeked out and there was nobody in the
house. No zombies, none of my friends
either. I think the zombies left since there
was nothing to eat. I am afraid all my
friends are zombies now.

Then I found Esther. I cried and cried.
They ate her, and left her body on a table
downstairs with stuff hanging out
everywhere. She was sort of my new
mommy. I loved her. I cried so much! I
found her diary in the attic.

Going on without her is so hard! I miss her.
I miss my real mommy. But I can read
Esther's diary and learn more about how to
live, and I can write about my life in the
diary too. That little book was the most
important thing to her, next to her picture
of her little brother Tommy.

I have lots of things in this house to help
me. I have food. I can learn how to cook. I

have shotgun bullets. Wait, they're called
shells, I remember now. I shot my first
zombie yesterday. I've never shoot a gun
before. It hurt my shoulder so bad like
Esther said it would, but I got him.

I want to fix the front door if I can. But it's
so heavy to lift. I am doing what Esther told
me. She said to stay away from zombies
nomatter what.

Somebody please help me. I'm only eight. I
don't want to die. I am so scared. I don't
know how long I can live alone. I don't
know *how long I can live…*

Jolene

Epilogue

Note that this Epilogue has spoilers for the story, so if you haven't done so yet, read the story first…

Originally, I had no intention of writing a zombie story. Believe it or not, it exists in support of a large Halloween party I threw in October, 2010. It really worked out well, much better than I intended. The point was to create a "background story" for the party. Every professional haunted house or theme park ride needs a background story for its theme to "live" in. I created the story around what the party was going to be like, and I changed the party to fit how the story was evolving.

A little background on me: I own a company that makes a product that plays back audio, video, lighting, and animation, and has built-in show control, that is used for theme park attractions and rides, as well as casino shows and the like. I have a lot of experience working on theme park attractions and haunted houses as well, and take my theming very seriously. The purpose of the party, other than having fun, was to market this product via demonstration, inviting guests who were customers or would-be customers, and later using pictures and videos as additional marketing. What's great is, one can do this while still inviting personal friends. It worked out really well and sales post-party paid for the party many times over.

Once I had decided to make the party a zombie party, I knew that the right way to do any serious themed party or haunted house, was to make a backstory as described above. I started by writing concepts down, that I might use solely for my own use, in making the party have a cohesive theme or possibly to include a paragraph or two in the party's program. I decided that it would be better to have the guests know the story before arriving, and came up with the plan below.

I worked on this party from May 2010 to October 2010, first every once in a while and then finally in September down to 7 days a week 10 hours a day. .

I wrote the ending of the story, day 15, first. I knew that I wanted the story to end with

Esther being alone in the worst possible position, with everyone in the story dead but Esther, and the reader not knowing if she lived or died. In the original party invite, I had told guests that they MUST come dressed as zombies or they wouldn't be allowed in. I hired a bouncer to ensure this. Then I had my daughter, who was about Esther's age in the story, dress in old clothes, and wrapped her around and around with clear packing tape, and then once thickly layered, I cut the clothes and tape off of her which left a mold that I filled with plaster of paris to the back half of the mold and discarded the front. I then added boots, fake hands, and hair to the mold, and lined the mold with food-grade silicon, and filled the "Esther" mold with food — spaghetti for intestines, port rib rack for the ribs, meatloaf in the legs, and so on. My assistant filled her head with a brain-like dessert. Esther was "dinner" and zombies were coming, but they had no idea of course.

I had invited guests prior to two weeks in advance of the party in order to have the guest list complete by the two week mark, and then, I started sending out Esther's

Diary day by day via email without explanation and without asking the guests. They just got it in their inbox one day at a time, with day 15 arriving the morning of the party.

As I wrote the story during the remaining two weeks, I already had a huge amount of the theming done, such as boarding up the windows, surrounding the front of the house in chain-link fence and making a front gate, and surrounding the back yard with 4x8 vertical plywood panels. I then continued to add story elements about things that were actually at my house, the "compound". In some cases I added things to the house that I had decided to write into the story, such as Esther's bunk bed, and the bunk below hers. The subplot in the story where Jack shoots John in the head on the back deck was added because I was using the back deck as a construction area, and had accidentally spilled some of the blood red paint on the deck. I started to clean it up, but decided to leave it and add that story element, knowing I would eventually take care of it after the party.

As I continued to write days of the diary, I added people who had RSVPd to the party INTO the story. Most, but not all, of the characters in the story were originally named after, and had general characteristics of, real people, who were attending the party. The only characters that weren't real people were people who would die in the story and not become zombies in the story, and Jolene, the lone survivor.

It wasn't long before I was getting feedback from guests saying, "Oh my gosh, what a great story, I can't wait to see what happens to Esther tomorrow," and, "I can't wait to see what happens to MY character tomorrow."

It built a tremendous amount of interest in the party, and it was exciting and motivating to me as well.

There are three main points to how strongly this story affected the party.

The first is that normally when you go to a party in costume, whether as a superhero villain, a vampire, or Frankenstein's Monster, you don't expect to be *held accountable* for who your character is. I hired actors to play humans in the front yard fighting against the zombies trying to get in. When guests went to go through the broken-down gate into the corridor to head towards the front door, they would yell at them and fire fake shotguns at them. The shotguns were plastic but had wireless triggers on the gun trigger that would trigger my company's product, and speakers concealed as crates in the front yard behind the actors would blast out large sound effects of real shotgun blasts, each time a slightly different cocking sound and blast. It really shook up the guests to go through a narrow fenced-in corridor being fired at from one side and an actor zombie on the other reaching at them through the fence. I covered the ground with bags and bags of used shotgun shells I picked up from a shooting range, so everyone was stepping on them and sliding and trying to get through the corridor. It was really a sight.

The second point is that upon arriving to the party, the guests had no way of knowing that the "compound", my house, was exactly the way the story described it to be. The gate, the corridor, the smashed-in front door, the back deck with Esther's bunk bed and 55 gallon drums, the balconies, and even the garage inventory where Michael died…all was there to greet people. People recognized things. I couldn't believe my eyes when I saw people queuing up to take a cellphone picture of Esther's bunkbed. What in the world are they going to do with that picture?

The third point is that when guests saw that Esther was sprawled out on the dining room table, filled with food, it dawned on many of them that they were the zombies in the story that were once her friends, and now were going to eat her. To most this was just a sort of "wow" (as some later explained it to me). A few were momentarily actually bothered by it, and a few said they "just couldn't eat Esther after reading about her for two weeks." How interesting the mind is and how it works! Bryan came up with the name of "Esther", and her full name "Esther Allison Timee", which was only written in the story once, Esther's last diary entry. Her initials and last name are supposed to hint at "EAT me", a lovely Easter Egg that I don't think a lot of people got.

For those who are interested in what else I did at the party, I'll list things I can remember here. Not all of these things tie in to the story necessarily, so I'll list them here at the end:

I actually made an FM radio broadcast that repeated a message a very short distance from my house, and people were asked to tune in the broadcast that night on the way to the party. I had to buy an FM transmitter, and I simply had the broadcast loop. The broadcast matched what Brad King on KPRR supposedly said.

Because I lived on a cul-de-sac, and most of the people on the street were going to the party, I asked my neighbors if it was OK to take up the entire street for the party. We lived in the mountains, so it was quite easy to get away with what I did. I wanted it to look like a typical zombie apocalypse highway where people had abandoned cars. I staged both of my cars, one off to the side. My Dodge Charger I took the spare tire/rim to my friend who owned a mechanics shop and had him take the tire off the rim. Then I put the rim back on the car, with scraps of rubber from a blown truck tire I found on

the freeway a month earlier. It looked like a
blowout. I parked my Jeep up on the
embankment just off the street so that it
was very vertical. I also borrowed my dad's
truck, and replaced the hood with a
smashed hood of the same model I got at a
junkyard for almost nothing. The paint
didn't match exactly, but it was dark outside
and no-one noticed the difference. The
hood was only four bolts – so it was easy to
swap. I put the smashed hood up at an
angle, and parked the truck right into a
lamppost I own mounted on a piece of
wood, so that it appeared bent in the front.
Then I put a fog machine underneath the
car with the output going up a tube right
next to the radiator, and put a speaker there
too, which played a sound effect of an
overheating and steaming radiator. When
the fog machine and sound effect were
controlled together, that effect was really
cool – it really looked like the truck had
crashed and its radiator was overheating. I
bought lots of suitcases and a toy tricycle
from thrift stores, and strewn them around
the road like people abandoned them, and
put bloody handprints on some of them.
Lastly, I stacked tires without rims and put a
propane flame effect (no I'm not going to

explain pryo effects – do NOT try this at home, I learned from experts) coming out the top, and placed these several places on the road and my driveway. It very much looked like the tires were on fire, especially because you couldn't see that the propane tank was actually in the stack of tires. The entire road was surreal, with cars strewn everywhere, some crashed, smashed, and on fire. There was trash, newspapers, luggage, and toys everywhere.

I removed my front door off the hinges, and built a new one that was the same exact size with the correct trim, then smashed it. I could have purchased a real door to do this with, but it seemed easier to smash one that I knew how it was constructed on the inside. Bryan and I built it, then smashed it in above the second hinge up, put bloody handprints all over it and re-hung it.

I hired two actors to fire at the guests as they came up the driveway and went through the corridor. They had black plastic shotguns that I had modified to have a trigger that sent a wireless signal to my show control product that played back a shotgun blast sound effect out speakers that were directly behind the actors. The speakers were hidden inside crates with a false side that was acoustically transparent. I also had a cocking sound effect before the blast. Every time the actor would fire the shotgun, it would pick and play a cocking sound effect before picking and playing a shotgun blast from a real shotgun. The next time would be a similar set of sounds from the same type of shotgun. The other actor had a different "set" of shotgun blast sound effects from a different real gun, so it legitimately sounded like two different shotguns, but each firing was slightly different. It worked great.

I placed several speakers around the house at the ground level that played back zombie moaning sound beds. I recorded as many people moaning as I could talk into doing it, and then I made several sets of really long sound effects where the moaning was mixed together, and then looped them. There were 3 differently mixed sound effects from three different speakers. The back deck had 8 foot high plywood that you couldn't see through, topped with barbed wire and police red rotator lights. You couldn't see over the fence, but you could hear the zombies moaning behind it, from a speaker behind each west, east, and north wall, respectively. It was really eerie to hear.

Additionally, we made a surveillance "station" on the back deck, which is in the story, which actually contained my product, audio amplifiers, and other real equipment really being used, plus TV monitors that you could view from the back deck. We put three fake cameras on the top of the wall on the back deck, the west, east, and north walls. The fake cameras ran cables to three video monitors on the "station" that played a really long loop of video surveillance footage from that "camera". To do this, we made three different films a month earlier. I was actually one of the actors myself as a zombie wandering around outside the wall. We positioned the real film camera for each film exactly where the fake ones were during filming, so when you saw the film footage on the monitors, you were seeing the exact same thing you'd really see if the fake cameras were real, with the addition of the zombies. The trees overhanging the walls and the film even matched up. It was very convincing.

Bryan and I filmed an additional film of Johnson and Blake on patrol being attacked and Blake being turned into a zombie, and then Blake turned on Johnson. We had four total films being played back from my product at the station.

On the plywood on the back deck walls, I spray painted several things and later wrote them into the story. It was supposed to be the residents of the compound venting. One of the things I spray painted was "ALL HOPE IS GONE", based on the Slipknot album of the same name. One weekend we were doing construction and my daughters were helping, my youngest daughter came out of the house and sat in a chair and just stared at that writing. I think it sunk into her what it meant. I also wrote elsewhere "Yesterday my wife killed a zombie. Today she became one. Tomorrow I may have to kill her. Soon I may kill myself." This I later incorporated into the story with Michael and Rose.

I put a Scheduler chalk-board on the wall by the front door, and listed the names of the characters of the story and what they were supposed to be doing. My oldest daughter noticed that her character had gone out for firewood and didn't come back. The expression on her face when she saw that was really great.

As mentioned earlier, John's brains on the back deck were really a big red stain of paint "blood" that we had spilled.

At random times during the party, I would have my product set off an "alarm" where I had a recording of voice announcements where there was a breach and I would turn on the red spinning lights for a period of time. I had two different effects that would coincide. On one wall on the back deck I had a pneumatic cylinder "bang" on the wall like zombies were trying to get in, at the same time my system made the audio of the zombies groaning loader and added one distinct louder zombie to the mix on-the-fly. The other effect on a different wall I had two fake zombie arms mounted to two different pneumatic cylinders and they would slowly rise above the wall, and the "alarm" would go off.

I wanted to do something special with the guests eating. I really badly wanted those military style metal plates that have places to put small servings of food, but the cheapest I could find was $11 each, and I needed to keep it around $1 each, for the over hundred guests that would come to the party. Ultimately I found a company that was selling as surplus junk two hundred Delta Airlines serving trays – dark gray trays that looked somewhat industrial for $100 for 200, which was perfect. I put plastic silverware in three different dark green ammo cans. I love theming. I later sold those same trays for $75 on Craigslist, so I really only paid $25. You wouldn't believe how many hours I spent trying to find the right plate to serve food on. It's one of those things that for some reason I felt really strongly about.

I built Esther's bunk bed and several other props, and borrowed 55 gallon drums, filed them a third with sand and put real firewood in them and lit them during the party.

I also built two different wall-mounted "cases" that were wooden cabinets with "BREAK IN CASE OF ZOMBIES" on the front plexiglass, and inside were a plastic

shotgun and a machete or crowbar in each.
The first one I left intact. The second one I
intentionally cut the plexiglass with a jigsaw
and took out the shotgun, as if someone
had smashed it. I then mounted them on
the wall inside the house, and for fun, I
cooked a pan of candy glass, smashed it and
put the shards inside the broken one, so it
looked like the broken plexiglass. Every
once in a while during the party I would
reach inside in front of people and grab a
piece of the candy glass and eat it. Fun!
Got some great jaws dropped on that one!

I also hired my friend's classic rock cover
back that everyone loved. My daughters
and I sang a Halloween song on stage too.
It wasn't a zombie song, but it was still fun.
I hired a bartender and of course the
featured drink was…wait for it….The
Zombie.

We made a piñata that was supposed to be
Rose's torso, which looked great and was
fun for guests to smash with a baseball bat.

The last thing I'd like to say, is how it felt to
me planning and implementing this party. I
started by boarding up the windows in May

of 2010. As I lived in the house every day for the next five months and kept making it more "compound" –like, and the last two weeks writing the Esther diaries, it was so very dark emotionally, even though I was otherwise in a really great place. I couldn't avoid it. It was actually depressing just being there. It definitely added to the feel for the story sitting in the same "set" as the story and writing about it while there. It's hard to explain, there was such a sense of despair and dread while working on the party props and such, and programming the show. I was also writing a chapter or two of the story each day. Sometimes I would get up from writing shaking. I hope that comes through in the story.

I hope everyone enjoyed the story and party as much as I enjoyed creating them.

Cheers.

Jeff S. Long

If you wish to receive updates on releases of this and other works, please request to join the mailing list by emailing jeffslong.author@gmail.com and visit my

Facebook page
http:/www.facebook.com/jeffslong.author

I am considering writing a sequel to my
Esther story if there is enough enthusiasm
for it.

Additionally, my non-fiction book on
professional themed parties, which will
include pictures and detailed information on
the zombie party, as well as a previous
"Goth Alice in Wonderland party" and my
upcoming Pirates of the Caribbean party, is
already in the works.

I may release a book on the pirate story as
well. I've already obtained permission to
borrow props from the original Pirates of
the Caribbean movie. The party will
revolve around a more historically accurate
story, rather than around the Disney
film/story, but the props will be great none-
the-less. Having worked on the Pirates of
the Caribbean ride at Disneyland helps…

Jolene lives….

www.ingramcontent.com/pod-product-compliance
Lightning Source LLC
Chambersburg PA
CBHW072148130726
47909CB00004BB/1264